1956 AND ALL THAT

A memorable history of England since the
WAR TO END ALL WARS (TWO)

1956 AND ALL THAT

Comprising everything you can remember and
including: 9 Prime Ministers, a Butler and
432 facts not contained in Irving
Wallace's *The Book of Lists*

by
Ned Sherrin
M.A. Oxon, Barrister at Law

and
Neil Shand
Matriculation (Exemption)

illustrated by
William Rushton
(Gent.)

MICHAEL JOSEPH · LONDON

First published in Great Britain by Michael Joseph Ltd
44 Bedford Square, London WC1
1984

Sherrin, Ned
    1956 and all that.
    I. Title   II. Shand, Neil
    828'.91407   PR6069.H459/

ISBN 0 7181 2479 0

Typeset by The Word Factory, Rossendale, Lancs.
Printed in Great Britain by Hollen Street Press, Slough, and
bound by Hunter and Foulis, Edinburgh

CONTENTS

Errata
For Precedent read President throughout
President read Precedent throughout

COMPULSORY PREFACE

(THIS MEANS YOU)

'History is not what you thought. *It is what you can remember*. All other history defeats itself.'

The great truth which lay at the core of Sellar and Yeatman's authoritative history holds true today, qualified only by the fact that it is possible to remember even less of recent history than of the remote past. Also, there are less Kings and Queens to go round.

Sellar and Yeatman charted faithfully Great Britain's progress as Top Nation, conceding ultimately that the Palm had passed to the United States of America. This volume seeks to establish that in the years since the WAR TO END ALL WARS (TWO) Great Britain has continued to be Top Nation, but with a subtle change: no other nation is now aware of this.

N.S.
N.S.

CHAPTER 1

WAR TO END ALL WARS (TWO)

The first date in the History of the World since 1956 is 1945 when the WAR TO END ALL WARS (TWO) stopped. This war was fought because Neville Chamberlain, a cautious man who never left home without his umbrella, waved a scrap of paper and promised everybody a Piece in Our Time. The German leader, A.

Rising gamp

Hitler, a Bad Man who owing to eccentric German ideas about klass was only a Korporal, took him at his

9

word and grabbed a piece of Austria, most of Czechoslovakia and all of Poland.

This was his attempt to make Germany Top Nation (*Uber Alice* in German) though most German soldiers were *uber* somebody called Lili Marlene. He then turned round and took large pieces of Denmark, Holland and France. Most French people had drawn a line called *Les Deux Maginots* past which Hitler was not supposed to go. However he went round it and the French ran away, with the exception of the French *pièce de résistance*, Odette Churchill, the illegitimate daughter of Winston Churchill, the new English Prime Minister who was famous for inventing a cigar which was as big as Neville Chamberlain's umbrella. He was affectionately known as Winnie and had only two fingers, which he frequently showed in a V sign to prove he wasn't Monty's double.

Battles of War to End All Wars (Two)

The battles included:

the Battle of Biggin Hill: we won 259–10;
the Sinking of the Bismarck: 6–1 to us;
the El Al Campaign – in which the Eighth Army, stealing a march on the previous seven, defeated the German Afrika Corpse. The English Tommies, Dickies (see Earl Mountbattenborough of Burma) and Harries were paid special allowances for fighting in hot climates. These were known as Desert Rates.

Other Obstacles

Apart from Hitler, Winnie's main opponent was General de Gaulle, also known as Gladys the Cross-Eyed Bear of Lorraine, a very tall French refugee who started a Free French Restaurant in London where the food was better than in British Restaurants. He refused to let Winnie eat there because he considered his Siren Suit to be improper dress, his inclination to smoke his large cigars in gourmet surroundings disgusting and because he did not like Winnie's habit of sticking up two fingers when he was handed the bill (*l'addition* in French, because they always add a bit).

'. . . as we say in English'

11

Oratory

Winnie pooh-poohed the German or Naahrzee threat in a series of talks to the nation, which included the memorable phrase:

> 'We will fight on the beaches, in the air and on the playing fields of human conflict for never have so many owed so much to some chicken and some neck . . .'

When the Germans heard this they put Adolf Hitler on their wireless; but we could not understand what he was saying so he was defeated.

The Americans

The Americans came into the war late. This is because their clocks are behind ours. Their main victories were on the Halls of Montezuma and the Shores of Tripoli.

The Russians

The Russian leader, Joe Stalin, was a pheasant plucker from Georgia (*See* Carter, Chapter 21) who now wanted to make Russia Top Nation, but his persistent attacks of indigestion meant that he had to have regular purges and couldn't give his mind to it.

CHAPTER 2

PEACE

The outbreak of peace was signed in Germany on Looneybins Heath (no connection with Edward Heath, *passim*) by General Montmorency who wanted the whole thing finished with so he could go off into the jungle with Chairman Mao and share his thoughts.

'Who are you doubling for?'

The difference between war and peace was that in the war you knew who your enemies were. The outbreak of peace was followed by two days of celebration:

1) VE Day
2) VJ Day

These days inevitably led to a day of mourning which was called:

3) VD Day

War Trials

In Nuremberg, all the surviving Naahrzee leaders were put on trial which was a chance for the Allies to get their own back on the people who had been a trial to them during the war. They included Herman Goering, Albert Speer, Albert Schweitzer, Von Papen, Von Bulow, Von Eggut, Von Two Three and Rudolf Hess who was sent to serve a life sentence with the Spandau Ballet. Adolf Hitler, Joseph Goebbels and Martin Bormann were missing, presumed dead (though Martin Bormann turned up later in Argentina under the assumed name of General Belgrano Galtieri).

Some Good Things

Peace brought some Good Things:

1) the lights went on in London once again, so the

famous song 'I'm Going To Get Lit Up When The Lights Go On In London Once Again' no longer had to be sung;

2) exports improved, especially to America. Their soldiers, known as G.I.s after their commander, General I'senhower, instituted a primitive bartering system with the British natives exchanging nylon stockings and chewing gum in return for young East Anglian girls. Many of these were later sent back and those that weren't were frequently passed on as good as new to other Americans;

3) General de Gaulle went back to France.

The General Election

Another result of peace was a General Election in which a grateful nation showed Winnie their appreciation by electing as Prime Minister Clementine Attlee – not to be confused with Clementine Churchill, Winnie's wife. The chief reason for Winnie's defeat was that he kept using his war-time speeches as an election address and calling the Labour Party a *Naahrzee Jestapo*. This confused the voters who were afraid that he might follow this by sticking up two fingers at them as well. So they sent Winnie off to build stonewalls, paint Lord Beaverbrook's olive trees and make Iron Curtains so that we couldn't see the Russians who had been Our Friends, but were now Our Enemies.

15

In the new Asperity Britain, where everyone was short of everything and short with each other Clementine's speechmaking style was more suitable than Winnie's since he rarely said more than 'Yes' or 'No'.

In-trays are outré

However, England was now a place *Fit for Heroes to Live*. Indeed you had to be a hero to live there. Although words like:

a) Blitz
b) Second Front
c) Gas Mask
d) Doodlebug

had disappeared, other words like:

a) Rationing
b) Ersatz
c) Utility
d) Coupon
e) Blackmarket (*See* Brixton, *passim*)

were still current.

The Labour Government

All the members of the Labour Cabinet were called
Bevin or Bevan. They included Ernest Bevin, Aneurin
Bevan, Sir Stafford Cripps Bevin, Hugh Dalton
Bevan, Herbert Morrison Bevin and, the most junior
of them, little Harold Wilson Bevan who never forgot
anything that happened to him during the next five
years and made sure that nobody else did either.

Together they all invented Nationalisation – a
scheme for taking away businesses from the privileged
few who made money for themselves out of running
them efficiently and giving them to a lot of people who
lost money for everybody else by running them in the
public interest, i.e. inefficiently. Among things they
nationalised were Coal, Steel, Railways, Gas,
Electricity, the Bank of England and the Doctors and
Dentists. The Doctors were particularly upset and
their rallying cry was 'The End is Nye', which was
short for Aneurin Bevan. He called them 'vermin',
which was long for 'rats'.

CHAPTER 3

KING GEORGE VI – A NICE KING

King George VI had had quite a lot of practice as King, having done it since 1936. To everyone's surprise the King got on very well with the Labour Government, especially with Clementine as they both spoke the same language (English); and since the King took a long time to say one word and Clementine never said more than two ('Yes' and 'No' – *see above*) audiences were mercifully short and a great many laws were passed during this time.

King George VI was a nice King who was lucky to have chosen a nice Scottish Queen who was called Elizabeth. Later she was known as *Queen Elizabeth, The Queen Mother*, but she could not be called that until her husband was dead and her daughter became Queen Elizabeth II. Queen Elizabeth (later the Queen Mother) was especially good at waving and smiling. Their two daughters had been called the Little Princesses and were now called Princess Elizabeth and Princess Margaret Rose Marie.

The Conservatives

When the Labour Party invented Nationalisation, the

18

Conservatives said it was a Bad Thing; but they did not invent anything themselves except Research. This was the idea of one man, R.A.B. Butler, who built a Research Department at Conservative Central Office. (For many years people did not realise the value of research, but by the late 1970s it had become England's only growth industry, employing millions of people, mostly in television.)

'I'm not just a pretty face, y'know'

The Sun Sets on the Empire

One of Clementine's biggest problems was to get rid of the far-flung outposts of Empire. (It had been comparatively easy to lose the nearer-flung ones like the Empires of Holborn, New Cross and Finsbury Park.) This was part of the subtle plan to make people think we were no longer Top Nation, when in fact we were. Also, now that Clementine had decided to make the pound worth less than half as much as it had been worth before, keeping up a far-flung Empire was an expensive business.

First of all he tried to get rid of India, also known as

the Sahib-Continent, but India did not want to Goa because that was Portuguese. To persuade the Indians, he sent Lord Mountbattenborough out as his Viceroy, with his nymphomaniac wife Lady Frequently Mountbattenborough, to scare off the Holy Men of India, Rhandhi, Ghandhi, Andhi and Pandhi, a group of itinerant sitar players know as the Raj Quartet. But the Indians had a Wise Man, or pundhit, called Nehru, who made such good friends

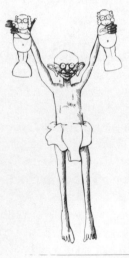

'Whoopee! I have two Dickies'

with the Viceroy that he was allowed to call him Roy, and even better friends with Lady Frequently, whom he accompanied to Jo-pharties and Curried Favour.

In the end the Sahib-Continent gave birth to two countries, India and Pakistan. This was known as the Parturition of India and Lord Mountbattenborough

20

was sent back to the Navy. As a reward for his services to Lady Mountbattenborough, the pundhit Nehru was awarded the style and title of the great Ram of Krutch. Rhandhi, Ghandhi, Andhi and Pandhi were assassinated nine days before Cinerama was invented, so it was many years before this memorable event was made into a memorable Motion Picture by Dickie 'Darling' Mountbattenborough, the old man's illegitimate son.

The Jaffacado Incident

Another part of the Empire which Clementine wished subtly to lose was called Palestine. When Palestine only produced oranges it was simple, but since the invention of Grapefruit, Avocado pears and Sharon fruit, which no one knew how to eat for a long time, life had become complicated. Here the patriots who wished the British to stay were called Ben Gurion, Ben Begin the Beguine and Ben Dovah, who later went to Tangier, changed sex and assumed the name of Golda Meir, thus becoming the first Palestinian to go abroad and come back a broad. Unfortunately, she still looked like a man, which was a Great Disappointment.

Shangri-Lanka

In Ceylon the name to conjure with was MRS BANANADANANADANANARIAKE and the only problem was pronouncing it. Once this had been solved and the Island re-named Shangri-Lanka, it went quietly.

21

Into Europe

Both Clementine and Winnie wanted to make better friends with the rest of Europe, especially Germany as many people were beginning to think that we should have fought the French not the Germans in the WAR TO END ALL WARS (TWO). To help the German Government, which was still in Bad Odour (a small German Town), the British Government organised the Berlin Air Lift to fly in fresh air and fly out de fetid air and to help the two main architects of German Industrial Recovery – Sir Stafford Krupps and the man who introduced British Summer Time to Germany (so that they could work as hard as we do), Konrad Add-an-hour. An important step forward was taken when all the Foreign Ministers of Europe went to Brussels and signed the Mannikin Peace which lead to NATO.

Konrad Add-an-hour

At Home

The Chancellor of the Exchequer, Doctor Dalton, had to resign because his budget leaked all over Westminster. Sir Stafford Cripps, who was leak-proof, was made Chancellor instead. As he was not as good at Getting the Economy Going as his German counterpart, Sir Stafford Krupps, the Government thought up several new ways of cheering up the people.

1) Bread was no longer rationed. Unfortunately, this produced many fat people so the next year clothes rationing had to be abolished and skirts were dropped. This was called the New Look and, as more skirts were dropped, it was soon to lead to the New Morality.

2) Television was reintroduced at the Alexandra Palace, a royal home for which the King had no further use. The most famous television personalities were Bill and Ben the Flower Pot Men, Muffin the Mule, and E. Macdonald Hobley, a West Indian sprinter.

3) County Cricket returned bringing with it the introduction of sponsorship. The Brylcreem Cup was won over six successive seasons by Dennis Compton, who was then allowed to keep it and his hair.

4) The Government organised the Festival of Battersea so that the entire nation could be taken for a Free Ride. One result was Festival of Battersea Design, in which everything from ashtrays to council estates was made of Bakelite and

23

painted in bright colours. As Battersea is on the south bank of the Thames, the Festival was known as the South Bank Show. The surviving buildings are a permanent reminder of the horror and destruction which can be wrought on a city centre in peace time when a competent architect puts his mind to it.

5) However, the Labour Party's most successful diversion was to arrange the engagement of Princess Elizabeth to Philip – a young Greek Naval Officer who was the nephew (legitimate) of Lord Mountbattenborough. As a wedding present, the King made him Duke of Edinburgh so that he would feel at home, since Edinburgh is traditionally known as the Athens of the North. The wedding also inspired Princess Elizabeth's memorable catchphrase, 'My husband and I'.

Everyone's coming up Margaret Rose's

While Princess Elizabeth had only one husband, Princess Margaret Rose Marie had a Set. In keeping with the egalitarian mood of the times, these demob. suitors adopted proletarian names such as 'Billy' Wallace, 'Sonny' Blandford and 'Danny' Kaye. They were allowed to sing 'Princess Margaret Rose Marie, I love you', but not to go any further. (The American counterpart of Princess Margaret Rose Marie was known as Princess Margaret Truman and her best friend was Prince Charming Douglas.)

CHAPTER 4

THE FACE OF BRITAIN CHANGES

The Face of Britain had changed under the Labour Party. It now had free false teeth, free spectacles and a free wig. Although lots of British people disliked the New Look, lots of foreigners were envious and came to England to get some. This was the beginning of Denigration. In order to check Denigration, the last Labour Chancellor of the Exchequer, Hugh Butskell, had said that people should pay for their false teeth, spectacles and wigs. This had led to the Charge of the Health Brigade during which all the Bevins and Bevans resigned. So did Clementine, in the end.

More Elections

The Labour Party's new policy of unrationed Bread, Circuses, Festivals, and Royal Weddings was not a success, but there were several elections before they were turned out. One of these was in America and forty-three were in Italy. The Italian Prime Ministers, who kept taking it in turn, were Signors Fanfani, Fan-Tutti and Fan-Elloni.

The British Prime Minister was once again Winston Churchill. In America, where the offices of Prime Minister and Queen are combined, General I'senhower won, in spite of having Richard Millstone Nixon round his neck. His slogan, 'I like Ikey', appealed to the Jewish majority in the USA and he garnered the large black vote because his wife was called Mammie.

Communism and the Bomb

During the early fifties, the main problem was that so many people were 'Soft on Communism'. Most Soft on Communism were the Russian leaders, Kruschov, Malenkov, Molotov, Gromikov, Tretchikov, Dabitov and Nastikov.

Next most Soft on Communism were two spies. One was American and the other was British. They were called Hissov and Fuchov. They both gave American secrets to the Russians, but because Britain was pretending not to be Top Nation, we no longer had any secrets. Most of the secrets we didn't have were about A-bombs. They were known as A-bombs because to make one you had to split an A-tom. This was usually done on a South Sea Island called an A-toll, where all the scientists wore B-kinis. The big bang was A-tonic to its inventors. The successor to the A-bomb was the H-bomb. Luckily the secrets which Hissov and Fuchov gave to the Russians were all about the C, D, E, F and G-bombs which did not work. In fact, all the bombs were made by Germans and the reason that the

27

American bombs were better than the Russian bombs was that the American Germans were of a higher quality than the Russian Germans. The American Germans were called Teller, Oppenheimer and Newcastle Von Braun, who had anglicised his name after bombing London during the WAR TO END ALL WARS (TWO). (WTEAW (2) from now on, *ed.*) American bombs were made at Los Alamos and Los Paraguayos. Many Americans built small underground dugouts to escape from the bombs. Because of the family rows which ensued in these cramped quarters, they were known as Fall-Out Shelters.

Get bombed

Wars

It was not only families who Fell-Out. Countries did so as well since, with the judicious exception of Great Britain, many were striving to be Top Nation. After WTEAW (2) they made a treaty to have a series (known as the World Series) of small wars instead of WTEAW (3). The first of these was held in Korea which divided itself into two teams, North and South

Korea. It was something of a local Derby, but Russia and China played for North Korea and England and America played for South Korea. The English players were led by a relatively unknown branch of the Royal Family known as the Glorious Gloucesters.

The war went on for a long time and was a draw.

Emergencies

Wars which were too small to be Small Wars were known as Emergencies or Police Operations. The three best known Emergencies were:

1) *Cyprus*. Where the Prime Minister of the country was also the Domestic Chaplain and was called

A bleach of the priest

29

Archbishop Domestos. He was the leader of the Greek Unorthodox Church and had a weakness for a Turkish starlet called Donna Kebab. However, he repelled her because he had *Enosis* (Greek for bad breath) which chewing *Eoka* failed to cure. Uncivil war broke out and Domestos was exiled to the Sea-Shell Islands where he spent his time learning the *Kareoka*. His rival, Costa-Grivas, a Greek film director, married Donna Kebab who became so famous that many people, especially in Britain, named shops after her.

2) *Malaya*. Where the only Britons to fight were known as Virgin Soldiers.

3) *Kenya*. Kenya was the part of the British Empire where people went to get their Koffee. There was an awful lot of Koffee in Kenya – almost as much as in Brazil. (Kenya was also where the Ground Knuts came from.) The memorable Kenyan leader, Omo Kenyatta, resented his whiter-than-white name and wanted all Kenya to be black. As Flame Trees are Thika than water, he took to the jungle with his Bau Wau society, sitting around campfires (made by setting fire to settlers' camps) and singing native chants like, 'I Get a Kikuyu out of You'. The British did not like these songs and sent Omo to jail for exactly seven years so that he could be released just in time to become President.

Home Policy

Meanwhile, Winston Churchill was getting tired and

most of his time was spent worrying about the picture which the memorable artist, Graham Sutherland, was painting of him. One day, while Winnie was being painted, the King died and Princess Elizabeth, who was sitting on a Tree Top in Africa with her husband, became Queen. Winnie fell in love with her, but, as she pointed out in a kindly fashion, they were both married already so nothing could come of it. Winnie resigned of a Broken Heart.

Queen Elizabeth II: The Punters' Queen

The Coronation of Queen Elizabeth II took place in Westminster Abbey in the presence of Queen Salami of Conga – a Great Queen who endeared herself to the people because she rode to the Abbey through the rain

'All I can see from here is the Queen of Tonga'

in an open coach with Sir Noël Coward eating her lunch. The Queen's best Coronation present was the top of Mount Everest which was given her by Sir Edmund Spillsbury, who brought it to London personally assisted by his faithful bearer. This produced the first recorded royal conversation of the reign when the Queen asked:

Is that Sherpa Tensing?
To which Sir Edmund replied:
No, Ma'am, he's just flexing his muscles.

The Second Elizabethan Age

As nothing significant had happened since WTEAW (2), celebrated writers like A. L. Growse, Hugh Trevor-Dacre, Sir Arthur Pliant, Beverley Winn and Godfrey Nicholls all prophesied the Dawn of a New Elizabethan Age of Expansion, Endeavour and Excitement.

Much was expected of the Young Queen.

TEST PAPER I

(Up to the Coronation of the Young Queen)

1) Arrange the following Monarchs in order of height, weight and trustworthiness:
   a) King Haakon of Norway
   b) Queen Whilhelmina of the Netherworld
   c) Haille Delighted of Rastafaria

2) In the General Election of 1945 how many Generals were elected?

   (Calculators may not be used.)

3) Give a recipe for making an omelette without breaking an egg.

   (Powdered egg may not be used.)

4) Which was the loudest:
   i) The Beveridge Report?
   ii) The Atom Bomb?
   iii) The Population Explosion?

5) Describe in gory detail the deaths of the victims of:
   a) Dr Bodkin Adams
   b) John Christie

c) Haig
d) Douglas Home
e) Edward Heath

(Use red ink freely.)

6) Where did Britain recognise Egypt. Was it at:
    i) A Pyramid Party?
    ii) The Gaza Strip?

7a) Examine the following figures carefully:
    a) 12
    b) 9
    c) 6
    Does this sequence constitute a Liberal revival?
    (Be charitable.)

7b) Now examine these figures closely:
    i) Betty Grable
    ii) Lana Turner
    iii) Jane Russell
    iv) Marilyn Monroe

    (Do not touch.)

8) In North Borneo they introduced the principle of One Man One Vote:
    a) Who was this man?
    b) How did he use his vote?

CHAPTER 5

THE SIXTIES

The first date in The Sixties is 1956, when the world changed. Unlike the memorable Queen Elizabeth I, Queen Elizabeth II was not a man; however, there were certain uncanny parallels with the earlier reign. (Not to be confused with canny parallels which are confined to Scotland and are therefore altogether different.)

Uncanny parallels

1) The cultural life of the nation centered around The Royal Court of the Queen, in Sloane Square, and its chief minister, George the Divine. Here, Beards, Long Hair, Poets and Playwrights were as fashionable as they had been under Good Queen Bess. The most powerful group of Royal Courtiers called themselves The Angry Young Persons. They were angry because at first all their plays were only performed in kitchen sinks, but as they got more successful they were transferred to the West End of London. They included Kingsley Wesker, Colin Osborne, Arnold Pinter and Harold Braine – they

were called The Angry Young Persons after the titles of their most famous plays:

Look Back in Anger
Angry Jim
Roots of Anger
The Anger Taker
and *Anger at the Top*.

The two most famous characters were Cole Porter (*Look Back in Anger*) and Lord Joe Lambton from another Angry play, *Whips With Everything*. (*See* Norma Levy, The Seventies, *passim*.)

'Is there a plumber in the house?'

2) *The Presence of Philip*. Queen Elizabeth II had married Philip of Greece whereas Big Bess did not marry Philip of Spain.

3) *The Margaret Factor*. Just as Big Bess had to bear with her cousin Mary, Queen Elizabeth II had a troublesome sister, Margaret – who chopped Rose

Marie off her name but did not lose her head, except over the most famous fighter pilot of WTEAW (2), Group Captain Douglas Bader. The Queen pointed out that he didn't have a leg to stand on and exiled him to France.

The Suez Armada

This was nearly an uncanny parallel but not quite. A crisis was provoked by the wife of the Prime Minister, Antony Eden, who refused to let the Suez Canal flow

The Provok'd Wife

through her Drawing Room and thus became known as the Provok'd Wife. The Egyptian Leader, Colonel Nasa, after whom the American space programme was named, was attempting to ferry supplies of food through the Canal from the Great Pyramid of Pork Cheops. Unfortunately this contravened the dietary laws of the Israelis who asked France and England to send an Armada to stop it. This was very nearly a mistake because it would have made people realise we were still Top Nation. Fortunately, just as we were teaching the Egyptians a lesson, the Americans, who have never been keen on education, decided to change the rules.

New Rules

1) Only America can start wars.
2) All wars fought by other people are started by Americans who for some reason wish to pretend that they are not involved.
3) All wars shall be known as Peacekeeping Exercises.
4) All American wars should be fought as far away from America as possible unless they have to be fought in America's back yard, i.e. Central America.

Sir Antony Eden decided to resign as he was too old to learn the new rules. He took the West Country title of Lord Avon because his wife did not mind at all if that river ran through her drawing room.

CHAPTER 6

THE COMING OF THE CROFTER

Supermac

One central problem in politics at home was to distinguish between the Conservatives, whose philosphy was propounded by R. A. Butskell (formerly Butler), and the Labour Party, now led by Hugh Gaitler (formerly Gaitskell); so the Conservatives chose Harold Macmillan, a whimsical publishing crofter whose PR

Shaz-ahm!

people called him Supermac because he was more eccentric than any other politician of the day. Supermac had a walrus moustache and very bad teeth which he later passed on to another politician, Harold Wilson, who admired them. Macmillan was a great phrase-maker, whose most memorable saying came about as a result of a punctuation error. His secretary, John Wyndham, who was more interested in writing science fiction (*The Day of the Triffids*, *The Kraken Wakes*) than he was in transcribing Supermac's speeches, had typed out, 'You've never had it so good.' In fact, what Supermac had meant to say was, 'You've never had it – so good luck because you're not getting it now.' However, once he had said it it was too late to take it back, so he had to give people things like houses, jobs, Premium Bonds, and American missiles, which worked by unclear fission and had romantic names like Blue Funk, Brown Study, Strike me Pink and The Robert Bolt. They were stored on sanctified ground at the Holy Loch and many times a year crowds turned up to worship them.

Urban Overcrowding

One big problem in these years was traffic jams and overcrowding in the main thoroughfares. There were two opposing factions which cut across party political boundaries:

1) *CND*, which encouraged people to fill the streets, especially the road from Aldermaston to London.

This group was led by Bertrand Russell and his wife Jane, which is why so many people who were conceived on these get-togethers are known as Russell, e.g. Russell Harty, Russell Davies and Russell Grant.

2) The opposition was led by Sir John Wolfenden, who brought out a report specifically designed to clear people off the streets – especially in the Piccadilly and Bayswater areas. Instead of meeting one another and jamming these popular thoroughfares, they were encouraged to make telephone calls or sign up for French lessons which were supervised with rigorous discipline.

Abroad

FRANCE

General de Gaulle came out of retirement at his country home at Colombey Les Deux Julio Iglesiases and proclaimed himself President for Life or Eternity, whichever was the longer.

He made the French plant lots of Golden Delicious apple trees, a secret weapon which he hoped within twenty years would bring about his Principal Ambition, the economic collapse of England.

CUBA

Supermac recognized Castro – he picked him out because he was the one wearing green fatigues and smoking a big cigar. The Americans had insulted him by calling him Fido – Russia's poodle.

'This is my Rubik Cuba'

RUSSIA

Relations between Russia and America were not cordial due to an American decision to send an aeroplane over Southern Russia to steal secret Armenian jokes. The pilot, Tyrone Powers, was shot down by the Russians and flown to Moscow. His luggage turned up in Vladivostock. The Russians were so angry when they heard Supermac telling secret Armenian jokes to the United Nations in New York that they banged their desks with their shoes, and refused to meet any American in Paris – not even Jean Kelly or her sister, Grace.

CHINA

Chairman Mau Mau and Prime Minister Chou-on-Gum exploded an A-tom bomb, but because it was Chinese two hours later they had to explode another one.

'Anyone want to come into the jungle?'

The Americans ignored the Chinese and spoke only to Madame Kash-mi-Cheque, widow of an earlier Chinese leader, General Kash-mi-Cheque, who was living in Formica, a little island off the mainland. As she found this very boring, she spent most of her time touring the world stirring up trouble and becoming known as the Great Wail of China. She changed the name of Formica to Try Wan On, which is what she was always doing.

At Home

CLAWS FOUR

This was an early attempt by the Labour Party to make a series of self-destructing Disaster Movies. *Claws One*, *Claws Two* and *Claws Three* were very unsuccessful; but *Claws Four* was Big Box Office and was memorable because of Hugh Gaitler's rallying cry, 'I shall fight, fight and fight again'. Although he meant that he would fight for the Labour Party, successive generations of politicians have interpreted it to mean that they should fight, fight and fight each other. (*See* Wedgwood Benn, 80s, *passim*.)

AN EXPLOSION IN THE ARTS

The excitement generated by the Royal Court of Queen Elizabeth in Sloane Square was now spreading throughout the length and breadth of the land. The Angry Young Persons, who were already a little older and a lot richer, had now been joined by the Noisy Young Persons, who were much younger but even richer. They were mainly performers who swing to and fro – Rocking and Rolling, as it was called – in front of large crowds in small coffee bars or in Big Cinemas where they could break up the seats. In America, Bill Bailey, who never came home, set the fashion with Marathon Sessions right around the clock, while a young protest singer called Pelvis Esley caught the current mood with his rebellious cry, 'Get off my blue suede shoes'. In England, the increasing violence of The Times was Mirrored in The Telegraph in the names of the performers, Steele, Wilde, Power, Fury. For all their ferocious nomenclature they were good lads at heart and cherished ambitions to become all-round entertainers and buy their mothers semi-detached houses in Epping Forest.

Another example of the cultural explosion was the plethora of Gossip Columns. Here the great figures of the time chose historical pen-names like Henry Fielding, William Hickey and Paul Tanfield and chronicled the good works of socialites and philanthropists like Lady Docker and Diana Dors. They were temporarily abolished by Lady Penelope Gilliat acting on behalf of H.M. The Queen.

T.V. – A LICENCE TO PRINT MONEY

The history of Television is divided into two parts: B.C. (Before Commercial) and A.D.F. (After David Frost). Television had originally been invented by Bogie Laird who was looking for something to kick to

'You are going to sleep . . .'

45

relieve nervous tension; however, he found himself lulled to sleep by flickering images on a small screen and realized that he had invented not only television but a product called The Grove Family, which Groucho Marx called a Sopiate for the Masses.

Under previous Monarchs only the Royal Mint (a homosexual by Royal Appointment) was allowed to print money; but under Queen Elizabeth II, anybody could apply for a licence. The people who were best at it were a group of aristocrats led by Prince Littler, the Queen's cousin, who divided the country into provinces which superseded the old county boundaries and had foreign names like Granada (Spanish), Rediffusion (French), S.T.V. (Lithuanian) and others which were as easy as A.B.C., A.T.V. and E.T.C. In these provinces, the Lords Lew Thompson, Lew Bernstein and Lew Grade reigned supreme. Anyone who opposed them was imprisoned in Harry Alan Towers.

Watching these developments with a critical eye was a Canadian lawman, Marshall Macluhan, whose motto was Not The Medium (of T.V.) But The Massage, and who started up a chain of massage parlours with the enticing motto 'Buttock Slapping Good'. He had a brief period of Glory but did not seriously challenge Prince Littler, who was getting bigger.

Many new professions were created by television:

Newscasters. Young men from the universities gained fame and riches by the hitherto unattempted feat of reading words printed entirely in large capital letters which rolled before their eyes on a revolutionary device based on the theory of the old fashioned toilet roll. Particularly expert at reading toilet rolls were Ludovic Bosanquet, Christopher Robin Chataway, and the senior practitioner, Sir Bronco Trethowan, who further sophisticated the device by introducing small fluffy puppy dogs who pulled rolls of toilet paper across the screen. Because they did this so quietly they were known as Hush Puppies.

Monkees. These were similar to newscasters and were even more lovable. There were two famous American Monkees: J. Fred Muggs, who went on in the mornings and Bonzo and Reagan, a double act which split up when the real monkey went into politics. The English monkey was called Desmond Morris and was tended by David Mountbattenborough (legitimate brother of Dickie 'Darling').

Commercials. The main difficulty which the new Commercial Television had to overcome was to find programmes which were exciting enough to interrupt the artistically exquisite and very expensive new art form – the commercial. Memorable artists like Lord Miles of Puddledock and Miss Huw Wheldon were paid vast sums of money to compose memorable phrases like 'Go To Work On An Egg', 'Don't Forget The Fruit Gums Mum' and those haunting refrains, 'Murray Mints Murray Mints, Too Good To Hurry Mints' and 'You'll Wonder Where The Yellow Went When You Brush Your Teeth With Pepsodent'.

Satire. Satire was a more altruistic form of television which owed nothing to commercial greed and which the BBC, with high moral interest opened on Saturday nights in order to close the pubs. It was therefore the direct brainchild of the BBC's first Director General, the calvinist Lord Hugh Carlton Reith, whose efforts to raise the moral tone of the nation had been inspired by his vision of the moral decay he had witnessed in the cabarets of Berlin in the thirties. He appointed a Methodist parson, the Rev. David Paradine Frost, to lead the hymn singing and soon everyone was singing about him.

Wilkommen

Bienvenu

Welcome

Zu Kabaret

Au Cabaret

To Cabaret

The Old Age of Supermac

The strain of keeping from the world the secret that Britain was still Top Nation was beginning to make

Supermac behave oddly in his advancing years.

1) He refused a special honour created for him by the
   Q.E.II. in recognition of his services to politics.
   She wanted to make him a (K.O.T.L.K.) Knight
   of the Long Knives, but he declined.
2) His health began to deteriorate when he went to
   South Africa and caught a cold from the tre-
   acherous Wind of Change.
3) He began to lose his hearing as a result of a new
   series of deafening reports:
   a) *The Kinsey Report*. This went off in America
      and had the effect of making people have
      more sex all round the world. The bangs
      were terrific.
   b) *The Denning Report*. This was caused by the
      Perfumo bang – the English reply to Kinsey.
      The Minister of Defence, John Perfumo, was
      a pacifist who embraced the popular phrase
      of the day, 'Make Love Not War'. He also
      embraced Christine Keeler who was a
      diplomatic bag at the Russian Embassy. In
      the memorable phrase of her friend, Handy
      Nice-Davies, 'Well, he would, wouldn't he?'
      This so upset Supermac that he was prostate
      with grief and his doctor, Lord Denning,
      ordered him to retire, looked after by his
      faithful manservant, Vassal, at his country
      home at Crichel Down.

CHAPTER 7

LORD HOME /
SIR ALEC DOUGLAS HOME

Two Prime Ministers for the Price of One

Lots of people wanted to be the next Prime Minister because it was a Good Job. Most people wanted R. A. Butskell except Lord Quintin Hogg, whose famous bell-swinging displays whilst skinny-dipping at

'We're a dyin' breed, y'know'

Brighton had earned the decade the title 'The Swinging Sixties'. Nobody wanted Lord Home, except Supermac because they both enjoyed peasant shooting. As everybody thought this was Supermac's dying wish they gave in. As soon as they had done so Supermac recovered. The country never did.

CHAPTER 8

A NEW PRECEDENT

While Precedent Kennedy and his lovely wife had occupied the White House it was known as Camelot because people did. The people who came included famous Artists, Musicians, Interior Decorators and Call Girls. Precedent Kennedy was the first Catholic Precedent which was why he had lots of brothers and sisters. He was the second son of a two-toilet-Irish family and his father had made his money in the twenties. The twenties were also memorable for the Charleston, F. Scott Fitzgerald and Inhibition. During Inhibition, Joseph Kennedy amassed a fortune with Speakeasy's where people loosened their tongues with Hootleg Booch. To mark the end of the twenties, many Wall Street bankers jumped off their own Tall Stories. The dents they left in the sidewalks were known as the Great Depressions.

However, Joseph Kennedy never jumped but lived on into the thirties. The thirties were run by Franklin D. Roosevelt, who did it from a wheelchair. He was a restless card player, always clamouring for a New Deal. In the forties he made Joseph Kennedy Ambassador to the Court of St James where his policy was:

a) to keep America out of the war;
b) if this failed, to bring them in on the side of Germany.

However, this was Nipped in the bud by two Japanese double agents called Tokyo Rose and Pearl Harbor.

When Jack became President he developed delusions of musical grandeur, standing on a wall in the middle of East Germany and shouting '*Ich bin Irving Berliner*'. Though he was elected for four years, being a young man in a hurry he wanted to do everything in One Hundred Days. This was made easier because he had the help of:

a) his Lovely Young Wife who did up The White House for him;
b) his Lovely Young Brother whom he made Attorney General with strict instructions to stamp out nepotism. And indeed there is no evidence of any Kennedy nephew being given a job during those One Hundred Days.

An Incident

The CIA attempted to capture Cuba by sending in a wave of inflatable policemen to block up the harbour of Havana. When the policemen were all captured, this became known as the Bay of Pigs. When they heard about this the Russians, who were Cuba's friends, sent a cargo of missiles to Cuba to blow up the inflatable policemen. However, as the Russian agricultural advisers who were accompanying them did not have enough puff they were sent back to Russia on Precedent Kennedy's advice so this was not a real crisis though everybody thought it was – at the time.

A Sad End

Precedent Kennedy's Precedency came to a sad end when he was shot in the Texas town of Dynasty by a group of American writers who wanted to write Long Books speculating on who might have shot him if they had not. The Longest Books were written by three Patrician Americans, Earl Warren, Count Basie and Duke Ellington.

CHAPTER 9

ANOTHER NEW PRECEDENCY

When Precedent Johnson succeeded Precedent Kennedy, the White House stopped being called Camelot because very few people came at all and if they did Precedent Johnson took them into the lavatory to talk to them and hold them up by the ears.

'Dallas has been good to me'

The Horticultural Precedency

Precedent Johnson encouraged a period of enlightenment and growth:

1) The Flower Industry boomed, especially in San Francisco where the Mommas and the Poppas only gave birth to Flower Children; some of these went to Radical Universities where they became plants for the CIA.

2) Sex was improved as a result of Precedent Johnson's campaign exhortation, 'Go all the way with LBJ'. Most people did.

3) As a result of horticultural and sexual liberation, drugs became increasingly fashionable at home and abroad. At home the Flower Children got stoned; abroad it was the American Embassies.

4) The Flower Children also proposed a new monetary system by which the Dollar would be replaced by LSD; but in spite of some imaginative trips this did not come about.

CHAPTER 10

HAROLD WILSON

The Swinging Prime Minister

Harold Wilson's most memorable achievement was to be the first Prime Minister to win the World Cup and two Eurovision Song Contests. This made Labour The Natural Party of Government (as opposed to the Liberals under Jeremy Thorpe who were known as the Unnatural Party of Government). Harold Wilson introduced a lot of policies none of which worked;

The Wizard of Drivel

however, as the people did, nobody worried.

Distinguishing characteristics of Harold's administration were:

1) A special language called Wilson-Speak of which the most memorable words and phrases were:

   a) 'First hundred days.'
   b) 'White heat of technology.'
   c) 'This will not affect the pound in your pocket.'
   d) 'Purposive', 'abrasive', 'pragmatic'.
   e) 'As I think I said at the Brighton Conference at twenty-three and a half minutes past two on Wednesday September twelfth . . .'

2) A Very Young Cabinet. This included Lavender Williams (22) Patronage Secretary, Kenny Lynch O.B.E. (21) Commonwealth Affairs, Harry Fowler (25) Home Office, Lord Joe Kagan (13) Foreign Affairs, Lord George Brown (29) Minister with Portfolio one day and without Portfolio the next, Barbara Castle (19) Minister for Flame-Haired Tempting.

3) By a bold constitutional stroke, Harold Wilson increased his power by appointing two doubles, John Bird and Mike Yarwood, who not only sounded exactly like him but made a great deal more sense.

4) He made his wife, Betty 'Betjeman' Wilson (*née* Keppel), Poet Laureate and published her diary every two weeks. Her most memorable poem was:

> Rain friendly bombs on Number Ten
> So we can to our cosy cot again.

Though Harold loves the pomp and show
I cannot wait to pack my small valise
And to the Warm and Welcoming Sillies go.

5) There were lots of new professions. The best new professions were:

a) *Photographer*. The leading photographers were Lord Antony Armstrong Bailey, Lord David Lichfield, Lord Patrick Donovan and Lord Terence Stamp.

b) *Fashion Model*. Usually known by nicknames such as Twiglet and the Prawn, who launched the fashionable disease, Anorexia Nervosa.

The thighs have it

59

c) *Boutique Owner*. Everybody had a boutique in Carnaby Street W1, or in the Swinging King's Road. Male customers, even if they were only buying a tie, had to be measured for size of inside leg.

d) *Footballer*. George was Best.

e) *Film Star*. This could happen overnight to anyone who was young, spotty, and had a provincial accent.

f) *Film Director*. See (e) above.

g) *Swinging British Films*. New Realism – see (e) and (f) above.

h) *Disc Jockey*. These were held captive in prison hulks moored off the shores of the island. From these pirate ships they introduced gramophone recordings of songs whose words could not be heard, with babblings which could not be understood.

i) *Pop Singers*. Troupes of young men, usually two, three or four in number with tight-fitting clothes and long hair, who sang the songs which could not be heard in (h) above. Two groups were pre-eminent:

(i) *The Rolling Stones*, led by Mick Jaguar, who had a Faithful girl friend whom he fed entirely on Mars Bars while singing 'I Can't Get No Satisfaction'.

(ii) *The Beatles*, who were discovered by Brian Einstein in Liverpool. Einstein called his second theory of Relativity 'The Liverpool Sound' and it made a lot more money than the first. The Q.E.II liked them so much that she made them Members of the Balham Empire. The Beatles made enough money to become very religious and went to India with their girl friends, Jane Ashran and Yoko O-Yes, to learn the secret of life from the Maharajah of Wishee Washee. The secret they learnt was that the Maharajah was very expensive and that it made him giggle all the way to the Bank of the Ganges.

British Breakthroughs

Under Wilson, there were many new inventions as part of the PM's White-Hot Technological Revolution. Some disquiet was felt by far-sighted politicians who felt that these advances might result in foreigners realizing that Britain was still Top Nation after all.

1) *The Torrey Canyon*. This was a ship built to shovel silt away from the Prime Minister's holiday home on the Silly Islands.
2) *Betting Shops, Casinos, Bingo*. These were all run by George Raft who was not allowed to come into the country to do it, so he handed the responsibility to J. Arthur Rank who hosted bingo sessions in ruined cinemas and churches where mystic chants like 'eyes down for a full house', 'fifty-seven, all the varieties' and 'clickety-click, sixty-six' inspired the faithful.
3) *Washing Machines*. These were invented by John

61

Bloom to make life easier for all the women who were now going out to work in order to earn the Higher Purchase money to buy a washing machine invented by John Bloom. Unfortunately, when everybody had a washing machine he was unable to sell any more and went bust. He was put on trial but the Q.E.II said she did not want to wash his dirty linen in public and deported him to America.

New Homes

1) *Ronan Point*. This was a thirty-storey block of flats which was cleverly converted into bungalows overnight.
2) *Halts, Junctions and Sidings*. Because of the shortage of houses, the Government appointed Sir Thomas Beecham to find some. His solution was to close down many railway lines, thus freeing ticket offices, waiting rooms, and left luggage stalls to be bought by people who wanted to live above their station.

Moral Climate

Another threat to Britain's subtle strategy was that she began to lead the world in an enlightened attitude to morals, largely thanks to the work of a dumpy and unremarkable Midlands housewife, called Fairy Lighthouse, whose subtle campaign methods appeared to oppose liberal legislation while in fact

'Hello, I am the Fairy Queen!
I am absurd but not obscene!'

giving the movement greater impetus. Single handed she achieved:

a) *Abortion*. (Not for herself.) She brought millions of pounds of much needed foreign currency into the capital by her catchy slogan, 'London is the Abortion Capital of the World'.

b) *Homosexuality*. Fairy Lighthouse was not entirely successful here. Her ambitions had been to make homosexuality between boys of all ages compulsory; but she only succeeded in making it legal between consenting adults.

c) *Divorce*. She introduced a new divorce law by which no one could stay married for more than two years, but this was not passed because as very few people did anyway, it would be a waste of time.

d) *The Pill*. She opened a chain of sweet shops selling sugar-coated pills to young girls who did not want to have babies. The girls who took these pills were called Smarties and the ones who did not were called Pregnant. (*See* (a).) The worldwide repercussions were immense and in Malaya the rubber industry collapsed.

Crime

1) Infuriatingly, Britain once again found herself leading the world, especially with the most famous crime of the century. *The Great Train Robbery*, as masterminded by the arch criminal Dr Beeching and his henchmen Bruce Reynolds and Ronnie Briggs. Between them they stole 2.6 million trains. The robbers were captured but the trains were never recovered, and are believed to be in a secret numbered siding in Switzerland.

2) *The Kray Brothers*. After the hula-hoop, Ronnie and Reggie were the most fashionable Krays. With their colleagues, Charlie Richardson and his boys, they gave parties for film stars and politicians at The Blind Beggar public house. The cabaret was usually an eccentric dance act known as 'The Mad Axeman', but when the neighbours complained about the noise of tearing finger nails, cracking knee-caps and other high-spirited japes, they were arrested and sent to prison for a very long time.

This was known as the Smoke Abatement Act, or Cleaning Up London.

3) *Murder*. There were two sorts of murderers – those who did it before the Abolition of Capital Punishment and those who did it afterwards. Most memorable in the first group was John Reginald Halliday Christie who tried to murder Ludovic Kennedy. His home at 10 Rillington Place had so many dead bodies in it that had he not been done for murder he would have been sent down for overcrowding. (*See* Rackmanism.)

Most memorable in the second group were The Moors Murderers, Lord Longford and Myra Hindley, who were allowed to go on seeing one another in prison.

4) *Spying*. Britain still had the best spies despite having exported three of the top ones to Russia. The ones that were spying on us were better than the ones who were spying for us, and so were awarded the Lonsdale Belt. The ones who were spying for us were given long holidays in Russia.

CHAPTER 11

DARKEST AFRICA

Throughout this decade, the British continued their enlightened policy of getting rid of the Empire in spite of the opposition of most of Africa. Proof that we did this sort of thing better than anybody else was offered by the ham-fisted way in which Belgium tried to get rid of her Empire. It was only a very small Empire, devoted to tribal dances and called the Conga. When the Belgians pulled out, a struggle developed between the captains of two rival formation dance teams, Patricia La Rhumba and Moise Tshstompe who put

'Lumumba?'
'Only in the mating season'

his foot down and insisted that it took two to Katanga. The United Nations sent in Des O'Connor Cruise O'Missile, an Irish journalist, to suggest a New Fangled Katanga. The rival dance teams soon lost their amateur status and were called Mercenaries. The competition continued for several months and people were very unkind to each other.

The most memorable formation dance call was, 'Any nun here been raped and speaks English'.

The British did not allow formation dancing and got rid of its Empire by not letting the countries be painted red on the map any more and by giving them new names like:

Ghana
Botswana
Guyana
Bhwana
Banana
Manyana
Ipececuanha

so that no one had any idea where they were.

This not only got rid of the Empire but also spelt the end of triangular postage stamps.

There were two exceptions:

South Africa. Ever since the Bore War, South Africa had vanted to be German and the Government introduced Goose Stepping vhich they called 'putting your best foot voerward'. Most of the time they put it voerward on top of black people. They were Varster than the other African countries and left the Empire before the Empire could leave them. The measure by which they distanced themselves was called the White Rule and when they left the Empire they called themselves Apart-ites.

Rhodesia. The Rhodesians were not as quick as the Bores, nor did they have as much gold or diamonds. Their leader was called Ian Smith (a very boring name) and as he had only one eye he led them the wrong way. He tried to be an Apart-ite too; but he wasn't quite boring enough and kept meeting Harold Wilson and his beautiful Chief of Protocol, Lavender Williams, on ships in the Mediterranean. This was a good choice of rendezvous as both sides were all at sea.

CHAPTER 12

WARS, UPRISINGS AND INCIDENTS

A Short War

The best war of the Decade was also the shortest. It lasted only six days which is only one day longer than the average test match. Because of this it was called the Six Day War. The two sides were Israel versus Egypt, Syria, Libya, Jordan, Saudi Arabia, Iran and Iraq. It might have lasted longer but Golda Meir, the Israeli leader, looked so much like Precedent Lyndon Johnson that the Arabs thought they were fighting America and gave in.

. . . and on the Seventh Day She rested

A Messy War

The Vietnam war was left over to the Americans by the French. While the older European countries were trying to get rid of their Empires, America was trying to acquire one and they were very grateful to the French for giving them an opening. Unfortunately, the local inhabitants did not want to become Americans, especially one of their leaders, Ho Chi Minh; he had been a waiter at the Carlton Hotel in London and when tourists refused to tip him, he had become very Hannoyed. Despite this setback, America continued to ship in modern amenities like phosphorous and napalm, supersonic Phantoms and Supersabres, exotic cocktails like Mighty Mouse, Bullpup, Sidewinder, Zany and Puff the Magic Dragon. As they began to take effect it was called 'zapping the Cong'. Unfortunately, the more cocktails they imported the less the local population liked them.

Meanwhile, the visiting Americans were sticking to drugs and appearing on television back home, which upset their friends and relations. Most upset was L.B.J. who decided to retire. He was replaced by Richard Nixon who on the advice of his friend, Henry Strangelove Kissinger, killed thousands more South East Asians which won Henry a Nobel Peace Prize.

Revolting Students

This was a direct result of the post-war baby boom (*see* Beveridge Report). England was worshipping the cult

70

of youth. (As one older statesman said, 'A British Youth has always been a cult to me.') Again, the world followed England's lead realising the source of their inspiration.

Student Leaders

Most of these were educated at the London School of Demographics (LSD). They included:

1) Tariq Ali, known as 'The Greatest', whose motto was, 'sting like a butterfly, float like a bee'.
2) Vanessa Better-Red-Than-Dead-Grave, the tallest demonstrator whom many students looked up to.
3) Daniel One-Arm Bandit, who organised the revolting French students who took over a Paris theatre with the cry, 'Roll out zee Barrault', to the tune of an Old English drinking song.
4) In America the protest movement was faithful to that country's show business traditions in that all the subversives were either double acts – Stokeley and Carmichael, Eldridge and Cleaver, Nichols and May, Sonny and Cher and Lord and Taylor – or large groups – the Chicago Seven, the Boston Twelve and the Indianapolis 500.
5) In Northern Ireland the charismatic young leader was a cricketing fanatic known as Bernadette of Lords and her Apprentice Boys.

At the end of the sixties, Harold Wilson bowed to student unrest (not to be confused with naked 'streaking', another political phenomenon of the sixties known as 'student undressed'), and lowered the voting age to eighteen, only to be confronted by another phenomenon, 'youthful ingratitude'; the newly enfranchised voters turned him down as the right man to run the seventies and elected in his stead, Edward Heath, a grocer from Broadstairs.

TEST PAPER II

(The Sixties)

1) Was Supermac:
   a) A dynamic Prime Minister?
   b) A luxury Gannex?
   c) A Scotsman who changed his knickers in telephone booths?

   (Be sensible.)

2) Did Esso Blue refer to:
   i)   Happy Motoring?
   ii) An early porno movie?
   iii) A member of a sponsored Oxford or Cambridge boat race crew.

   (Be sporting.)

3) Was the song 'There will never be another you' a reference to:
   a) Nancy Mitford?
   b) A protest about the cutting back of sheep pastures?
   c) A Secretary General of the United Nations?

   (Be lyrical.)

4) John Profumo was a renowned model maker. Describe his most famous model.

(Be scandalous.)

5) Was the condition 'Tired as a Newt' discovered by:
   i)   Desmond Morris?
   ii) The infant Ken Livingstone?
   iii) Lord George Brown?

(Be temperate.)

6) Which of the following could a fourteen year old not do:
   a) Vote?
   b) Fight?
   c) Become a pop millionaire?
   d) Have sexual intercourse?

(Be precocious.)

7) Was Hastings Banda:
   i)   An African leader?
   ii) Half a brother of Mrs Bandaraneiki?
   iii) A South Coast resort's answer to the Beatles?

(Be significant.)

8) Was the Master of the Queen's Musick:
   a) Sir Lionel Bart?
   b) Sir I'm Backing Britten?
   c) Sir John Vassall?
   d) Sir Tom Driberg?
   e) Sir Godfrey Winn?

(Be gay, but sensitive.)

9) Explain the difference between a building society and a permissive society and the difficulties in obtaining a mortgage from either.

(Wear an Abbey habit.)

10) Had Mr Kruschev been assassinated instead of President Kennedy is it likely that:
    i) War to End All Wars (Three) would have been declared?
    ii) The Russians would have opened another twenty-seven salt mines?
    iii) Mrs Kruschev would not have married Mr Onassis?

    (Set squares and red squares may be used.)

11) Did the Hon. Mrs Gerald Legge become:
    a) Lady Lewisham?
    b) Lady Dartmouth?
    c) Lady Spencer?
    d) Barbara Cartland?

    (Don't be a Burke.)

12) Was a 'desirable flat':
    i) An apartment in Grosvenor Square?
    ii) A convenient puncture?
    iii) Twiggy?

    (Search your mammary.)

11) If you went out with two pounds in your pocket and bribed three Metropolitan Policemen how much change would you have left?

    (Be cheap.)

12) Was a Maryquant:
    i)   A measure of quantity?
    ii) A measure of quality?
    iii) A flaw in one's make-up?

(Use a mirror.)

13) Subtract 007 from MI5 and divide by BBC 2.
    (Answers should be shaken but not stirred.)

14) If the Edinburgh Trattoo was a march pasta of Italian waiters, what were:
    a) The Sinking of the Aretusa?
    b) The Secret of San Lorenzo?

(Be fashionable.)

15) How far could your hair come down and your skirt go up without revealing your sex.

(Be ambivalent.)

CHAPTER 13

THE SEVENTIES –
THE WOMAN'S DECADE

During the seventies, Britain's strategy of pretending not to be Top Nation really came into its own and an amazingly convincing illusion of failure and decay was created.

Just as the Youth Cult had dominated the sixties, so the Cult of Femininity informed every aspect of public life in the seventies. As there were no memorable men during this decade (apart from a few memorable failures – *see* Heath, Wilson, Nixon, Bruce Forsyth, etc, *passim*), women became the symbol of the newly-floundering society. In tune with this transformation, the Queen's face appeared on all postage stamps, women won the women's tennis championship at Wimbledon thoughout this decade, and Princess Anne was elected Sportsperson of the Year, which pleased her new husband, consort and mount, Capt. Mark Fog-Phillips, who had always insisted that she was a jolly good sport.

Most Memorable Women included:

1) Germain Greer, sometimes known as Vanessa Red-grave, very tall Australian eunuch who gave a whole new meaning to the phrase Down Under.

2) Golda Meir, the very old Israeli who was no longer mistaken for Precedent Lyndon Johnson, because he had died.
3) Jane Fonda, an energetic American who did not find her true vocation until the eighties but who urged all right-thinking Americans who were fighting in Vietnam to stand up and be counted. 10,000 of them did and were shot.
4) Barbara Castle, the flame-haired temptress whose manifesto 'In Place of Wife' offended millions of conventional Trade Unionists.
5) Margaret Thatcher, blonde Member of Parliament and Junior Minister who made her reputation for courage and enterprise by snatching milk bottles from children's doorsteps. She then went on to quarrel with the unsuccessful leader, Heath, but later promised to bury the hatchet, which she did – in his back.

Other memorable women included Mrs Indhira Cartland, Barbara Ghandi, Shirley Bandaranike, Gloria Friedan, Betty Steinem and Barbara Windsor.

For years women had objected to men paying for their meals, giving up seats to them on buses and trains and opening doors for them. In response to their protests they were now allowed to take men out, to train losing racehorses and to be hammered on the Stock Exchange. In one respect, the authorities went too far and gave a woman The Order of the Bath which she took as a criticism of her personal hygiene.

CHAPTER 14

EDWARD HEATH –
A LAZY PRIME MINISTER

Edward Heath was principally memorable for smiling and shaking his shoulders. This was because he found it very hard to move his vowels. He also liked playing the organ, but insisted on playing everything in a major key because he could not stand the miners. He liked to go yachting and was always greeted by his crew with the words, 'Hullo, Sailor'. He finally lost the job because he refused to work more than three days a week and was always going off into Europe on holidays.

'I'm having trouble with my vowels'

CHAPTER 15

HAROLD WILSON – II
THE SEQUEL

When Edward Heath resigned nobody really wanted Harold Wilson to be Prime Minister. However, he thought he was the best man for the job of getting the country back on its feet, having previously brought it to its knees. Being short-handed, he ran the Government with his Chief of Protocol, Lavender Williams, who frequently did the honours. Thanks to her Social Contacts, Harold got to know many Trade Union Leaders and owners of Slag Heaps and asked them to No. 10 Downing Street for beer and sandwiches. Late into the night they would discuss the country's financial problems and very late one night they came up with a plan to revolutionise the World Bank.

The plan was to merge:

The Italian LIRA with the German MARK to produce THE LARK.

The Japanese YEN with the French FRANC to produce THE YANK.

The Czech GROAT with the Indian RUPEE to produce THE GROUPEE.

And the Greek DRACHMAE with the English POUND to produce THE DROWNED.

The suggestion was that you could get four GROUPEES for a good YANK and the DROWNED would be allowed to float.

The Chancellor of the Exchequer, Dennis Healey, considered this scheme evidence that there had been too much beer and not enough sandwiches at Number 10 and rejected it.

Time heals all wounds, Healey wounds all the time

The Trade Unions.

Crucial to the British Grand Strategy was the role of the Trade Unions who loyally fostered the impression around the world that Britain was a nation of lazy, workshy shop stewards.

Pre-eminent were the miners, who to a man laid down their tools and picked up their copies of *Richard III* and recited 'Now is the Winter of our Discontent'. Top reciter was Joe Gormless, who spoke so beautifully and caused so much disruption that the Q.E.II gratefully made him a lord.

The only industry short of strikers was football.

After the miners, the next best strikers were the car workers, who were constantly threatening the management of British Leyland that they would put the boot in. To which Sir Mini Michael Edwardes retorted: 'Good. Now if they'd only put the engines and the seats in we'd be back in business.'

Dockers, postmen and railway workers were also loyal strikers, though in the case of railway strikes people could rarely detect any difference between them and normal working. Trade Unionists who didn't strike, sat in – with the exception of the sewage workers.

The Common Market.

Another subtle British ploy during these years was a half-hearted attempt to 'get into Europe', where six countries had got together to open a market on a piece of ground in the centre of Brussels called The Common. Three reasons for delay were fabricated:

1) The cost of a day return on a Cross Channel Ferry.
2) The absence of a Chunnel.
3) A reluctance to learn foreign languages.

The reason for this delay was that the British thought that if we were a part of Europe there would be:

a) No place to go for a holiday abroad.
b) No more twin towns.
c) And no more bombing raids on Hamburg.

Eventually, the continental countries pleaded with us to join, pointing out all the beautiful scenery there was to be enjoyed – scaling the butter mountains and wine surfing on Lac Burgundy and Lac Valpolicella. The British holidaymakers who did not find this sufficiently exotic were forced to invent Miami in America, a seaside resort at the foot of the Blue Rinse Mountains.

CHAPTER 16

AMERICA

Richard Nixon – The Precedent Who Had It Taped

During the first two years of the seventies Precedent Nixon spent most of his time flying to Moscow or Cairo or Peking pretending to be an international statesman and trying to get rid of his nickname, which was 'Tricky Dicky'. He was abroad so often that his fellow Americans began to wonder if he knew something they did not. The only places he did not visit were Vietnam and Cambodia, but he sent a lot of bombers in his place. (N.B. he did not go to Chile either but he sent the CIA – Cheap International Assassins – to pay a formal call on Señor Allende.)

When the time came for him to be re-elected, his main opponent was Edward Kennedy, a Bostonian who was married to Arianna Onassis. One night after they had been toiling in Martha's Vineyard, he drove home in a tired and emotional Ford Estate and asked for a loan from a passing country person to pay the toll fare. 'Lend a chap a quid, hick,' he said, to which the yokel replied, 'You'll miss that bridge when you come to it.' Kennedy was so discouraged that he withdrew from the campaign saying, 'I wish I'd learned to stand before I decided to run.'

This left Richard Nixon without an opponent but he still wasn't taking any chances and sent some plumbers in to flood the Democratic filing system, so that they couldn't find out who their new candidate would be. (He was in fact called George Can't-Govern and he was so dull that without the filing system, no one could remember him.)

Unfortunately, after Nixon's unopposed re-election, one of the plumber's sprang a leak which led to the White House where Precedent Nixon was recording his greatest hits for the Watergate label under his professional name, 'Tricky Dicky and the Ehrlich Men'. His backing group, who all sang beautifully,

'Testing, . . . **†*‡§*!? . . . testing'

were Haldeman, Mitchellman, Magrudderman and John Dean, who was the first to leave the group and sing on his own.

The tapes were not a success:

a) Because Nixon held up their release.

b) Because people objected to the language.
c̀) Because one of them was faulty.

As a result, Nixon retired to Best Western White House, which rapidly became the Best Western Nut House, at In Clemente, California. Here he took daily walks to launder his money and spent the rest of the time lying on the beach, which made a change from lying in the White House. He later tried a come back on T.V. under David Frost's management – but only one of those tapes was any good so it came to nothing, although his fee came to quite a lot.

CHAPTER 17

THE REST OF THE WORLD

The seventies was a difficult decade for countries
without a woman leader.

Uganda

Nowhere was this felt more keenly than in Uganda,
where President Amin thought he was Queen of the
British Empire. In fact, he was simply a bad Precedent
who had lots of time to kill so he killed lots of times.

His only redeeming feature was his love of animals,
particularly alligators to whom he used to feed
anybody who disagreed with him. Accordingly, many
of his opponents escaped to the west as handbags. In
the end, in a shameful display of ingratitude, the few
remaining Ugandan people threw him out and he was
last heard of living in the harem of Col. Godawful in
Libya.

Libya

Col. Godawful was the one man who was more

mad than President Amin, but he had the advantage of being very rich. His wealth came from Libya's two principal exports – oil and terrorists. (The principal import became hijacked aeroplanes after Cuba felt that their market had been flooded.)

'I said I am ad-libbing, not a mad Libyan'

The Rest of The Middle East

After the Arab-Israeli War II (known in Scotland as the Yom Kipper War) the Arabs got above themselves and started to make unfair profits out of the oil which we had discovered for them in the first place. Their attitude was so vulgar that they chose as their chief negotiator a man called Sheik Your Money Abaht, which he and they did in Saudi Kensington, the Saudi of France and Saudi California. They also charged so much for petrol that only they could afford to buy it. Many people predicted that their monopoly would be the death of Western Civilisation As We Know It and it was called Putting the Cartel before the Hearse. Henry Kissinger a senior American secretary who was always in a terrible state, shuttled to and fro to try and mediate, but whenever he missed his shuttle he left the Israeli General, Moshe Dayan, to keep an eye on things.

Greece

The Colonels who ruled Greece were officers but certainly not gentlemen. How could they be with swarthy, Middle Eastern names like Popadumalopolis, Karavanananalis, and Theodopolopolopolis. Their main crime was torturing people who could not spell their names; but being Colonels, they lacked imagination and denied themselves their most potent instrument of pain by banning the acting and singing of Melina Mouskouri and her husband Nana Mercouri, even on Sundays. In her spare time, Nana Mercouri became the Greek Marbles Champion.

CHAPTER 18

SCANDAL AT HOME

The Slag Heap Scandal

This was a very aristocratic scandal. It involved Lord Lambton who used to meet his slag above Earl Jellicoe in Maida Vale. When this troilistic exercise was discovered, Mr Heath took away the whip which so annoyed Lord Lambton that he resigned in a huff.

The Instant Custard Scandal

This was a greedy scandal. Reginald Maudling, who was a more Important Minister than Lord Lambton, had a weakness for custard and T. Dan Brown & Poulson regularly flew him in supplies from their custard factory in Malta. The police were able to pin the custard on Brown and Poulson who both had to do Porridge. Maudling got off because he had eaten all the custard and destroyed the evidence.

The Vanishing Pier Scandal

a) Following the fashion set by Southend, Brighton,

and Morecambe, Lord Lucan, a more fashionable Pier, disappeared leaving his wife, Annabel, wondering where she could find a new nanny. Since then, he has been seen in Australia and South Africa but is most probably living in sin in South America with Ronald Biggs.

b) John Stonehouse was not a Pier but he probably would have been if he had not disappiered. Being more common than Lord Lucan, he was not as good at it and ended up naked in prison having left his clothes on a beach in Miami.

The Peeping Pier

Lord Pornford, whose main hobby was visiting ladies in prison, found a new interest in the seventies when he organised a coach trip to Denmark for himself, Cliff

Lord Pornford

Richard and the Midlands housewife Fairy Lighthouse to go and see sex shows. When they returned, they came clean which was more than they could say for the sex shows.

CHAPTER 19

JAMES CALLAGHAN –
A PLODDING PRIME MINISTER

Harold Wilson had by now done a good job in persuading the world that Britain was on the skids and the only way he could think of furthering his aim was to step down and make way for an older man. The one that the Labour Party chose was James Callaghan, whose first job on entering Number 10 Downing Street was to open all the windows and let the smoke out. He found Harold Wilson a difficult man to succeed as he did not have:

a) A wife who wrote poetry or kept a diary.
b) A dog called Paddy.
c) A holiday home in the Silly Islands.
d) A funny raincoat.

However, he did have a son-in-law whom he made Ambassador to Washington, which was the most memorable thing he did during his tenure of office.

His most imaginative piece of statesmanship was to try to complete the freeing of the Empire which had been started by Clementine Atlee in the forties. Callaghan's plan was to liberate Scotland and Wales and give the countries back to the Scots and the Welsh, so he had a referendum. Unfortunately, there were many more Scots and Welsh in England than there were in Scotland and Wales, and they were afraid that a referendum meant that they would be referred back to where they came from, i.e. Scotland and Wales, so the plan failed. (N.B. This was called a Devolution which explains why so many voting papers were marked 'Start the Devolution Without Me'.)

Being a Labour Prime Minister James Callaghan was very keen on his Labour relations and spent a lot

'It's my Party and I'll cry if I want to . . .'

of time visiting them. He thought he had a special way of talking to Trade Unionists. He ran a special crash course for the members of his cabinet at a place called Grunwick in North London where Ministers could learn the language in six easy lessons. The most memorable phrases were Flying pickets, Secondary pickets, Mass pickets, Sticky wickets, Peaceful pickets (now obsolete), Working to Rule, Wild-Cat Strike, Worker's differentials and Concordat.

Because Harold Wilson had left him with a very small majority, Callaghan had to make friends with the

Liberals and their leader, the Boy David. He would have preferred to make friends with the Conservatives for two reasons:

a) There were a lot more of them.
b) Their ideas were much closer to his own.

However, this would have been breaking the rules and it would have taken all the fun out of politics.

CHAPTER 20

PRECEDENT FORD –
AN ACCIDENTAL PRECEDENT

Precedent Ford, an Accidental Precedent, got his job when he was promoted to Vice Precedent when Vice Precedent Spiro Agnew was found to have too many Vices. He was known as the Greek bearing away gifts. Precedent Nixon, having sworn once too often, said, 'I beg your pardon', to which Ford replied, 'Granted as soon as asked' and became Precedent, thus confounding at a stroke the ancient prophesy that Richard Nixon would never be able to sell the American people a second-hand Ford.

Precedent Ford was accident prone and the American People soon felt that they could not carry on with a Precedent who kept hitting women with golf balls and bumping his head on the Wailing Wall, and whose idea of a foreign trip was stumbling over the step of a Chinese restaurant. Above all, he could not walk and pronounce the name of Lyndon B. Johnson at the same time. This disqualified him from running which was just as well because every time he ran he fell over. When he stopped being Precedent, he and his whole family went into show business, except his wife Betty who founded a clinic for Elizabeth Taylor, Peter Lawford and Tony Curtis.

CHAPTER 21

JIMMY CARTER –
A NUTTY PRECEDENT.

After the Democratic Camelot of the Kennedy's, Americans were at first surprised and later disconcerted by the Disneyland of the Carters. Jimmy Carter started off as a peanut vendor and a dedicated family man. He naturally thought, therefore, that his family was the correct choice for First Family. 'Hi, I'm Jimmy Carter and I'm running for Precedent,' he used

'Ah've been born again again and it still ain't workin'

to say with engaging frankness and he continued to say it all the time he was in the White House.

Since he was so proud of his family he decided to give them all jobs and not have a cabinet.

1) Jimmy Carter's job as Precedent was taken by his wife *Rosalyn*, who was his First Lady if you didn't count a sixteen-year-old at High School in Plains, Georgia.

2) *Ms Lillian Carter*, his feisty old mother whose consuming passion was women's rights (hence her insistence on Ms before her name), and who ran the Peace Corps.

3) *Ms Amy Carter*, the Precedent's very young daughter, invented the idea of child's portions at White House State Dinners, and advised the Precedent on his policy with regard to the Atom Bomb.

4) *Billy Carter*, the Precedent's brother, rarely came to Washington but ran the gas station back home in Plains, Georgia, and made frequent buying expeditions to Libya, where his pawky Southern guile enabled him to circumvent the outdated Moslem distaste for alcohol. He told his brother he was going to the desert to dry out.

5) *Bert Lance Carter*, distant cousin, was Carter's Bank Manager back in Georgia. As a reward, he was appointed to a Senior Financial Post in Washington, but Something Happened and he went back to being a Bank Manager again.

6) *Cyrus Carter Vance* stepped into Henry Kissinger's shoes and disappeared.

7) *Jody Carter Powell and Ham Jordan Carter*, the Precedent's two favourite rapscallion young cousins, got into scrapes, experimented with cocaine and qualudes, peered down the cleavage of visiting ambassadors' wives and poured Amaretto and cream (a revolting southern concoction) over unsuspecting Washington women.

8) *Zbig Znew Zbzi Zinski Carter*, the Precedent's distant cousin, came from Warsaw and was a Polish joke.

9) *Andrew Carter Young*, the Black Sheep of the White House Family, was American Ambassador to the United Nations. His job was to explain American Policy at the UN, but as America had no policy at this time he used to say the first thing that came into his head.

America had no policy because Jimmy Carter was too busy jogging, going to church, cleaning his teeth and lusting after women in his soul.

CHAPTER 22

WORLD AFFAIRS

There were a lot of World Affairs during the seventies.

The Shah v. The Amapola

Persia was now called Iran to confuse it with Iraq. Persia was ruled from a throne of Peacocks by the Shah in Shah, the Lord of the Eastern Isles, the Emperor of His Rule, the Most High in Omnipotence, the Grand Vizier of the Gardens of Babylon, titles he had inherited from his father, Corporal Bert 'Majoribanks' Pahlevi. The Shah got a lot of money out of Iranian oil and a lot of pleasure out of torturing Iranian subjects. He was also a great patron of the Arts, commissioning grandiose monuments to himself and ambitious television programmes on the same theme. Technically, there were two sorts of Muslims in Persia at this time: the Shites and the Sunnys. He was not a Shite, though he often behaved like one, but he was popular in England because he bought lots of old tanks and guns and new Concorde aeroplanes which no one else wanted.

His principal enemy was a very old man called the

Amapola How Meini, who managed to live in Paris for several years without having any fun in that lovely city. This was because having fun was against his religion. Everything was against his religion except chopping off people's arms (for stealing) and legs (if you tried to run away). If you were caught committing adultery other bits were cut off.

Tragedy tomorrow, Khomeni tonight!

Perversely, the Persians wanted the crack of this sort of firm government and asked the Amapola to come home and give them a dose of it. So the Shah had to move out and the Amapola Quame back to Quom. Nobody who had accepted the Shah's hospitality in the past now wanted to give him house-room, except Anwar Sadat, the most important man in Egypt, who put him up until he died.

101

Sadat and Begin

Begin the Beguine, who had been living quietly in Israel since Chapter 2, got himself elected Prime Minister when all his opponents had died or been discredited. He and Precedent Sadat of Egypt both wanted to win a Nobel Peace Prize, so Precedent Sadat made an informal visit to Israel for the Eurovision Song Contest, which Israel won that year, and they both agreed to go on to stay with Precedent Carter's friend Camp David in Maryland. In order to qualify for the Nobel Peace Prize, they had to sign a paper agreeing to stop fighting. When they had done this they went to Stockholm and collected the money, and then, in the tradition started by the previous winners, Henry Kissinger and Le Big Thoe of Vietnam, they started fighting again.

'Let's sheik!'

Rhodesia

There were a lot of meetings, especially between The Rev. N'Dabaniga Sithole, Joshua N'Khomo, Robert N'Mugabe, Bishop N'Muzorewa, the Rev. Canaan N'Banana and the British Foreign Secretary, David N'Owen as well as Andrew Carter Young, who enjoyed going to Africa because it was fashionable for Americans to trace their Roots. N'Othing much came of all of this for the N'Moment.

The Rest of Africa

The rest of Africa was chiefly memorable for the war in Angora. This was called the Initial Conflict because it was between the FNLA and the MPLA, but it became confused when Cubans and Europeans were imported to fight on opposite sides and got the initials mixed up. In the end, the Cubans decided to go it alone and won. They now own Angora, which was a pushover not a pullover.

The Boat People

When the Americans left Vietnam, the South Vietnamese wanted to go too but the Americans did not want them to go with them so they had to get into boats and sail off into the sunset – hence their name, the Boat People – except for a few hundred who were flown to England in January and became known as the

Boat Show People. Many of the other Boat People are still at sea.

North Vietnam

Until the North Vietnamese won, China was On Their Side, but when the South Vietnamese lost, the Chinese thought the North Vietnamese were getting above themselves, so they invaded them. They were asked to withdraw but took a long time about it, which is not surprising since if the Chinese knew how to withdraw there would not be 900,000,000 of them.

CHAPTER 23

EVEN MORE MINOR INCIDENTS

Attempt to Nobble Princess Anne in the Mall

This was perhaps the bravest, not to say most foolhardy incident in the seventies. It was thought by many in the horse-racing fraternity to be a practice run for the later kidnapping of Shergar (a racehorse with similar features). On Princess Anne's previous formidable form the betting was 100-1 against the kidnappers so nobody cleaned up except the newspapers.

Cho-Patti Hearst and the Symbigidiotic Army

This was a Liberation Army whose avowed object was the Liberation of large sums of money from several banks. They forcibly enlisted the aid of Cho-Patti Hearst, who already had lots of money and therefore knew to which part of a bank to go to ask for more. They were so appreciative that they wanted to make love to her all the time; when she was rescued, she rejected her old boy-friend for a policeman who also knew exactly what to do in these circumstances.

The Spaghetti House Siege

Three West Indians held six Italian waiters hostage in Knightsbridge for 122 hours, refusing to release them until the Pope embraced the Rastafarian faith. Unfortunately, the Roman Curch was between Popes at this time (*See* The Religious Revival *below*) so no one could give the West Indians a definite answer and they surrendered.

His Hailleness the Rastafarian Pope

Three Mile Island

This was a true life incident based on a film, *The China Syndrome*, starring Jane Fonda and Jack Lemmon. It took its name from the height to which the A-tomic power station in question would have been blown had not Ms Fonda got there in time.

CHAPTER 24

THE RELIGIOUS REVIVAL

The seventies saw the burgeoning of New Religions and a lot of cults. Some were counterproductive, like the People's Temple in Guyana led by Trade Union Leader Jack Jones. This was a confused religion which required followers to commit suicide during their initiation ceremony. After all 9,000 of them had done

Transcendental money-making

this it died out. Many people wished that the same rites could be embraced by the Hairy Krishnas (who perversely had no hair), the Moonies, who paid their leader, the Rev. L. Ron Sunyan Moon, large sums of money to marry the first person he thought of so that he could go on living happily ever after. The other main leaders of new religions were Bernard Levin,

Malcolm Muggeridge, Barry Funtoni and Christopher Booker.

In the mainstream of religion this was a period of confusion since the leaders of the various Christian churches were trying to get together while most of their congregations were trying to stay apart. This was called the Economical Movement, because it was held to be cheaper to have one church for all rather than a lot of churches for one – which was the size of the average Church of England congregation at this time.

The seventies was a record decade for Popes, who included Pope Paul, Pope John, Pope John Paul, Pope John Paul the Second and Pope John-Paul-George-Ringo, the Beatle Pope, who flew all over the world by DC 10 and always kissed the ground in gratitude upon landing. He was the Polish Pope whose first command on his election was to order a second coat of paint for the ceiling of the Sistine Chapel.

CHAPTER 25

SPORT

The great sporting names of the decade were Benson & Hedges, John Player, Nat West, Gillette and Everest Double Glazing, who competed with one another for maximum coverage on the field and on the screen. As a result, the Corinthian Tradition gave way to the Macormackian tradition, in which you were not entitled to call yourself a true sportsman unless you had an agent, a business manager, a personal hairdresser, and a million dollar contract for endorsements of shoes in which you could run all the way to the bank.

Watch this space

One new game was invented in Australia, by the visionary Kerry Gold-Butter-Packer. Twenty-two men assembled at night under floodlights on an Astroturf pitch. They were dressed in brightly coloured costumes. They played a game in which some hurled a hard spherical object at others who defended three sticks with a wooden club. (The authors do not know what this game is called, but it certainly wasn't cricket.)

CHAPTER 26

1977

This is the third memorable date in this book because it saw the two most important events of this period:

1) The Death of King Pelvis Esley.
2) The Silver Jubilee of Her Majesty the Q. E. II.

Crowds of equal size gathered in London's Mall to watch the Queen passing by and in Memphis, Tennessee, to mourn the passing of the King who

Wreck and Roll

might have survived had the doctors around his deathbed been able to find a drug which he had not already taken. At his funeral, mourners had intended to play 'Shake, Rattle and Roll'; in the event, all they had to do was jiggle the coffin. However, he was buried in state – a terrible state.

The End of the Seventies

Towards the end of the seventies, people started putting things to right:

1) *In America*, Precedent Jimmy Carter kept falling down on the jog and giving interviews to *Playboy* magazine, which upset the Amapola How Meini who had not had sex since his sons were born. He therefore imprisoned all the Americans in Persia so that they could not have sex either for one year. As the Chinese ambassador to Washington pointed out, 'They'll miss the election.' As they could not vote for Jimmy Carter, he lost.

2) *In Great Britain*, James Callaghan had a holiday in sunny Guadaloupe with Jimmy Carter. When he got back reporters asked him what he was going to do about the crisis. 'What crisis?' enquired Sunny Jim, and called an election. Then he discovered what the crisis was. He had lost.

TEST PAPER III

(The Seventies)

1) Who would be disappointed not to get a standing ovation from their audience:
   a) The Pope?
   b) The orchestra at the Last Night of the Proms?
   c) The cast of *Oh Calcutta*?

   (Be virile.)

2) Is the newest Paris building called:
   i) The Pompidou?
   ii) The Pompidon't?
   iii) The Pompimaybe?

3) Was the Bermuda Triangle:
   a) A *ménage a trois* arranged by Janey Jones?
   b) A device for making a Stonehouse vanish without trace?
   c) A flight path favoured by Freddie Laker?

   (Be mysterious.)

4) Explain the point of decimalisation.

   (Use a parking metre.)

5) Discuss the premise that a guaranteed crash diet was an in flight meal on a DC 10.

(Use a black box.)

6) Conjugate the following in a future tense:
   i)   I MF.
   ii) We MF.
   iii) They MF.

(Be imperfect.)

7) Jimmy Carter was described as a 'one-term' Precedent. What was the one term most frequently used to describe him?

(Peanuts is not enough.)

8) Discuss the Trade Descriptions Act in connection with:
   a) Massage parlours.
   b) The Virgin Islands.
   c) An evening of Music with Barry Manilow.

9) If you were the Pope and you were suffering a Crisis of Conscience, would you call:
   i)   Your Confessor?
   ii) A Vatican Council?
   iii) Mark McCormack?

10) The Ayatollah is not a Shite. Refute.
    (Be fundamental or your answer will be chopped off.)

11) When Margaret Thatcher said, on becoming Prime Minister, 'I'd like to thank the one man

without whom this would not have been possible,'
was she referring to:
a) Saatchi?
b) And Saatchi?
c) Edward Heath?
d) Tony Benn?

12) Who said, 'One small step for man, one giant step
for mankind.'? Was it:
i) Neil Gagarin?
ii) Yuri Armstrong?
iii) Ronnie Corbett?

13) Estimate the weight of Lord Goodman and Cyril
Smith to the nearest ton.

(Be liberal.)

CHAPTER 27

THE EIGHTIES

The Second Industrial Revelation

As there had not been an Industrial Revelation for over a hundred and fifty years, Sir Clive Sinclair decided to have one. His revelation was a machine called a computer which only very young children could understand. As the older people could not fathom how it worked, they were unable to compete and had to do compulsory leisure instead of work. It was not that easy for the young people because although they knew how to compete they could not find anywhere to go and do it. (This was a very worrying time for the enlightened Government, which was brand new and which, in order to pay for all the leisure that people had to spend, needed the income from taxes which they would have received had the people who were at leisure been at work. There were a lot of these and the most expensive of all were the people who were at Her Majesty's Leisure.)

Her Majesty was still Queen Elizabeth II, though there was some doubt about this in one person's mind. This was Mrs Margaret Thatcher who had no clear idea why she was still called Mrs Margaret Thatcher and not Queen Margaret I or Good Queen Meg.

The Iron Prime Minister

The inevitable conclusion of the woman's decade was that a woman should achieve supreme power and also be on top, and so Margaret Thatcher became Britain's first woman Prime Minister. Known as the Blessed Margaret, she would certainly have been canonised

Queen Margaret I

but for her understandable ambition to be Queen. She was also known as the Iron Lady. Her first act on coming to power was to get rid of the Opposition. Accordingly, she dismissed Norman St John Stevas, exiled James Prior to Ireland and promoted William

Whitelaw to the House of Lords. As there was a lot of trouble with the Damp Course in Tory Headquarters, unsympathetic Conservatives were delegated to attend to it and earned the name 'Wets'.

Her burning ambition was to be known as the Prime Minister who abolished inflation,* following the advice of a former American slave called Milton Freedman. He was known as the Architect of the Black Economy, an idea which Mrs Thatcher, as well as a lot of other people, soon cottoned on to. His solution was so simple that a child could understand it. Unfortunately, Mrs Thatcher was a Grown Up; but as she treated all her cabinet like little boys (except Sally Oppenheimer whom she treated like a big boy) it did not matter. She told them quite clearly to stop inflation and they said we can only do this if a lot of people are not working. To which she replied, 'That does not matter as long as my policies are working.'

On the whole, she was more a philosopher than a politician.

* Inflation is what happens when a Chancellor of the Exchequer gets the wind up.

CHAPTER 28

CONSERVATIVE PHILOSOPHY

1) *A return to Victorian values.* This was difficult to put into practice since most houses had central heating, which left few openings for child chimney sweeps – and so the Youth Opportunities Scheme collapsed.

'Let them eat Sir Keith Joseph!'

2) *Bicycling.* Here, Mrs Thatcher's inspiration was a minor Conservative politician called Tebbit, who advanced the theory of the Pay Norm – this meant pay Norm and to hell with everybody else. He

learnt it at the knee of his father, a champion Olympic cyclist, who never got off his bike except to father Norm.

3) *Upward Mobility*. This was perhaps the biggest change in Tory thinking (apart from the concept of Tories actually thinking). In essence, the theory of Upward Mobility meant that people with titles, land and an old Etonian tie would no longer be considered for Government if there was a fat man with a double-breasted, chalk-striped suit, a bad accent and a background in public relations and double-glazing who wanted the post. Some experience in grinding the faces of the poor was also an advantage.

Conservative Philosophy in Action

i)   Do something appalling at home.

ii) Do something even more appalling abroad so the newspapers don't write about the appalling things at home.

iii) Give the editors Knighthoods for swallowing this device.

e.g., *Rhodesia* had been waiting for the crack of firm government for a long time and so Mrs Thatcher sent her fattest Minister, Sir Christopher Churchill, to sort out the warring parties – ZANU, ZAPU, HARPO and GROUCHO – on the principle that if he failed, he would not attend the independence banquet, he would be it. However, he did not fail but in a simple stroke of statesmanship changed the name of the country to Zimbabwe. This meant that Ian N'Smith, who had always n'sisted on a white Rhodesia, did not mind once it was called something else. All future African states will have the letter Z at the beginning of their name like Zimbabwe, Zaire, Zambia, Zouth Africa, Zudan and Upper Zolta. In recognition of independence, Queen Elizabeth II visited Zimbabwe, attended the Ideal Zoames Exhibition, and danced the blackbottom with any member of her Commonwealth Family who had anything approaching a sense of rhythm.

CHAPTER 29

THE ROYAL FAMILY

Prince Charles

An even happier distraction was Mrs Thatcher's search for a suitable bride for Prince Charles. She rejected Princess Astrid of Luxembourg, the Joan Collins Dynasty and the Three Degrees in favour

'I think one's undergoing the Third Degree'

of a simple country girl whose father owned Northamptonshire. The product of a broken home, Lady Di had been brought up by the putative step-Queen-Grandmother-in-law of the future King of England, Barbara Carthorse, and was generally held to be the Last Virgin Left in England. She was an infant teacher at the Pimlico Comprehensive School for Under-privileged Dukes and lived with three girl-friends in a mansion block for trapped aristocrats known as Earls Caught. Lady Di was also the spiritual leader of a large sect known as the Sloane Rangers, who wore green wellingtons and re-wrote old Beatles songs, changing the words 'Yeh! Yeh! Yeh!' to 'Yah! Yah! Yah!'

A romantic courtship climaxed in a railway siding near Swindon when Prince Charles gave a new meaning to the time-honoured phrase 'The Royal Male Must Get Through'. The Caught correspondent of the *Sun* news-paper, Fred Papparazzi, broke the news to a waiting nation and the young couple were married soon after during a Royal Variety Wedding at St Paul's Cathedral, starring Kiri Takenover and Spike Milligan. The performance was watched on forty million television sets in England, two hundred million television sets in Europe and four hundred million television sets in America. In Japan nobody watched as they were too busy making more television sets. Soon afterwards, but not too soon, the union (the only union to get Margaret Thatcher's approval) was blessed by a child, Prince William, who took a long time to arrive because he insisted on coming out with his hands behind his back, like his father and grandfather before him. When the infant Prince did arrive, the Royal gynaecologist slapped his bottom and instead of crying like other babies he gave a gracious wave. Prince Charles expres-sed a wish that his first- born should have all the things he never had as a child, like India, Pakistan and Tanganyika.

Prince Randy

Prince Randy, a helicopter pilot, had smaller ears than Prince Charles but a bigger chopper. A keen photographer and balletomane, Prince Randy mounted his most notable coup, Starkers, in Mustique, where he was staying with his Auntie Margaret Jones.

Prince Edward

Having failed all his exams, he was sent to New Zealand by Mrs Thatcher so that he could come back and get into Cambridge as an overseas student. Once there, he took up a lot of his older brother's hobbies.

Princess Anne

People had thought she was a Sulky Princess, but she was persuaded to talk to Cecil Parkinson on Australian television where she won all hearts by imitating Australians and revealing her wish to be a long distance lorry driver. This made her a Good Thing.

The Queen Great Grandmother

She carried on being a Good Thing without any help from Mrs Thatcher.

CHAPTER 30

AMERICA

Mrs Thatcher had a weakness for older men and in the new American Precedent, Ronald Raygun, she found a father figure who was even older than her husband. She liked to say that she had Precedent Raygun's ear, but unfortunately she found out some years later when he invaded Grenada that he was deaf.

Precedent Raygun was a film star Precedent whose co-star, closest confidante and wife was Bonzo, a chimpanzee who thought that the underprivileged were people who had never worn a designer original. Precedent Raygun was a copycat Precedent. He copied Margaret Thatcher in all her policies except one – it was her policy to sleep as little as possible and his policy to sleep as much as possible. On his bedroom door was a notice saying, 'In Case of Emergency, Do Not Disturb'. This meant that he did not have to do anything about incidents in Afghanistan, Poland, Nicaragua, or San Salvador.

Precedent Raygun's biggest triumph was to keep his hair whilst all around were losing theirs. America was used to colourful Heads of State, but even they had never seen one this colour – which was bright orange. Like Margaret Thatcher, Precedent Raygun was against Unions unless they were in Poland. The leader of the Polish Union (Liquidas) was an oversexed, Catholic shipyard worker from G'Danzig called Letch Lenska, whose sister, Rula, had hair the same colour as Precedent Raygun, which gave them something in common. Letch's other friend was the Polish Pope, who flew to see him whenever he felt a bit homesick.

Precedent Raygun had a lot of friends in Central America (which is the bit between North America and South America which most people did not realise was on the map until Precedent Raygun tried to blast it off it). He was most friendly with tribes of Gorillas in San Salvador, San Nicaragua and San Guatemala, because of the influence of his wife, Bonzo; her other friends were dress designers and hairdressers or shopkeepers' wives, like Betsy Bloomingdale, who was very smart and thin as a whip.

'Hell, Nancy, you should see the picture in the attic'

CHAPTER 31

COLOURFUL ENGLAND

Back in England, it was high summer and a riot of colour, especially in Brixton and Toxteth. These were select districts known as 'Ghet-tos' in the West Indian *patois* because everybody in the Carribean wanted to get there. A happy, simple people, they found England very cold, so they set fire to their houses saying, 'Dere goes de neighbourhood!' A judge called Lord Scarman was asked to find out how they could be kept warm so he wrote a long book and had thousands of copies printed. These he sent to Brixton so that they could be burnt instead of the houses. Only a few of the West Indian leaders, Rastus Farian, Reggae Farian and San Farian, preferred to keep the Home Fires burning.

CHAPTER 32

NORTHERN IRELAND

Meanwhile, Northern Ireland was in the grip of the fashionable dieting craze. To accommodate this, James Prior, who was particularly fat, set up state health farms called F-Plan Blocks where the guests could follow the Bobby Sands diet. Some of them found the regime too taxing, since it meant giving up lots of things, including living. The Irish leaders, Bernadette Devlin and Ann O'Rexia Nervosa, Shameless Hockey and Garret Fitz-Curling were against this; but the Catholic Bishop of Armagh, Monsignor Ian Paisley, was all for it and kept encouraging his supporters by leading them in the traditional Irish ballad, 'Knock 'em in the Old Falls Road'.

CHAPTER 33

THE FALKLANDS FACTORY

This was the only growth industry in the eighties, apart from competing. Mrs Thatcher and her friend Carrington of the FO, had been trying to sell the Falkland Islands to the Argentine for a long time because they felt they could not condone what the islanders got up to with their sheep. However, when the deal was almost done, Mrs Thatcher suddenly realised that the Falklands was the ideal site for the Third London Airport and told the Argentines to forget it. The Argentines were very upset, but Mrs Thatcher told them not to worry in the memorable phrase, 'Don't Cry For Me, Argentina'. This did not pacify the Argentine Leader, General Belgrano Galtieri (*See* Chapter 2, previously known as Martin Bormann) and Mrs Thatcher had to send in the Q.E. II and her son Randy, whose Task was to Force the Argentines to go away; but first she told Carrington of the FO to FO. We won because we knew more about the enemy weapons than the enemy because we had sold them almost all of them, with the exception of the Exception Missile, which was French and therefore unreliable and smelled of garlic. This was encouraging because it meant we would have a better chance of selling more weapons to the Argentine in the future.

Everyone back in England was very proud of Mrs Thatcher's Factory and no one ever made a speech without referring to the Falklands Factory in glowing terms. Indeed, when it was time for an election, the Falklands Factory was the principal reason for Mrs Thatcher's victory.

The Goose Green Step

CHAPTER 34

THE GENERAL ELECTION

Subsidiary reasons for Mrs Thatcher's Victory:

People To Whom She Was Especially Grateful.

a) *Michael Foot*, for all he did for the Conservative Party by staying on and behaving as though he was Leader of the Labour Party. His fashionable tailor, Ox Fam, his early morning aerobic walks, and his endearing mongrel, Paddy II, as well as his declared new Arms Policy (he promised to wave them about less in future) made him a much loved figure of fun.

b) *Tony Benn – The Incredible Shrinking Name*. Benn campaigned vigorously for Mrs Thatcher from his power base in Bristol, along with his disciples, Eric Heffer, Dennis Bolsover and Arthur Scargill, who was affectionately known as the Pits, and like Mrs Thatcher opposed the miners on every issue.

c) *Francis Pimm*, Mrs Thatcher's No. 1 and Secretary for Foreign Affairs. (Mr Michael Parkinson was her Secretary for Unfortunate Affairs.) Francis Pimm was not a good Secretary as he took dictation badly, so Mrs Thatcher slapped him down and all the masochists, of whom there were more every year, realised how much they wanted the smack of firm government and gave her a Thumping Majority to the delight of the Party Whips.

d) *Edward Heath*. Mrs Thatcher was very grateful to Edward Heath, for just being what he was; but then she always will be.

Newts at Ten

e) *News Knights*. This was a popular Television Game Show, hosted by Sir Alistair Day and Sir Robin Burnett, which gave Mrs Thatcher a chance to show the humorous side of her personality. The Rules of the Game were that Mrs Thatcher was asked a lot of questions and as long as she did not answer any of them she won the Major Prize, which was the whole country.

f) *The Women of Greenham Common*. This was the name of Mrs Thatcher's Fan Club, who sportingly waited until after she had been elected to go for a Cruise and so increased her majority.

Parties To Whom She Was Especially Grateful

a) *The Labour Party.*
b) *The Liberal Party.* The Liberals were led by 'Boy George' Steel, who followed in the tradition of Lloyd George and Boy David. They won ten seats in the House of Commons but this only gave them five MPs as the Member for Rochdale needed five places.
c) *The SDPP.* The Some Drink Plonk Party were divided because their leader, Woy Jenkins would not dwink Plonk but only the best claret. He was offered safe seats in Wugby, Wipon and Wuislip, but chose to stand for Glasgow Hillhead because at least he could say it without embarrassment. He was known as the Bad Oyster of Politics because he was no good if there was an 'R' in the month. After the Election, he stood down in favour of Dr Shirley Owen, who knew his 'Rs' from his elbow, but not much more.
d) *The Monster Raving Loony Party.* (*See* a, b and c above.)

Election Promises

Within six months, all the great Election Night promises had been broken, especially the one which went, 'Of course I'll marry you, darling.'

CHAPTER 35

THE NEW GOVERNMENT

This was the same as the old one but for three changes. Mrs Thatcher brought in John, Selwyn and Gummer.

It was known as the Banana Skin Government because Mrs Thatcher slipped up on several banana skins, e.g.:

1) One was dropped in the streets of Cheltenham by the British Head of the KGB, Sir Anthony Blunt. When Mrs Thatcher offered the unions a thousand pounds a head to pick it up they then dropped several more. The man dropping the most banana skins was awarded the Cheltenham Gold Cup, the Top Prize at the GCHQ.

2) Another was dropped by her son Mark on a lump of concrete in the Gulf. Mark's hobby was getting lost in deserts and he was fond of quoting the old Bedouin sore 'Greater love hath Oman'.

3) A man called Ken Livingstone – the head of the Greater Livingstone Council – dropped them all over London, which made it very hard for her to get about so she went off to the Winter Sports Funeral in Moscow, starring George Orwell and Christopher Dean, where she said 'Goodbye' to Mr

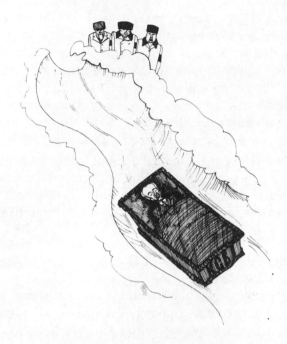

Go, Yuri, go!

Andropov and 'Hallo' to his even older successor, Mr Evrytinksdroppinov.

4) But the man who dropped the biggest banana skin was a Yorkshire Trade Union leader who was known as the Unacceptable Face of Coal Mining, to which end he combed his hair eccentrically to the far left to distract from the rest of his Unacceptable Face. Unbeknownst to himself, Arthur Scarface was being eaten away by a disease called Gormleymylitis, which manifested itself in its

sufferers with an unquenchable desire to bring down Conservative Governments, and he was preparing for retirement. He bought a large house in Sheffield, which he called *Dunstrikin'*, and surrounded it with a flying white picket fence. However, not all the miners were afflicted with Gormleymylitis and these men wanted to have secret ballets organised by Rudolf Nureyev. However, Arthur Scarface vetoed this, saying that:

a) Male ballet dancers were effeminate.
b) It was illegal to do it with a miner.

The collapse of the miners' union (NUMB) meant that all the other unions – NUPE, GRUMPE, SNEEZE and DOPE – gave up hope and collapsed too. Except for the Police Union – BOSSE – which became stronger and stronger.

Every time Mrs Thatcher slipped on a Banana Skin, people laughed. She did not like people to laugh at her, so she arranged for Prince Charles and Princess Diana to have another baby to distract them and to fill the many newspapers owned by the Australian newspaper typhoon, Sir Iris Murdoch, whose favourite song was 'The Times It Is A Changing'.

CHAPTER 36

THE SECOND ROYAL BABY –
THE ROYAL WEE.

There was a national competition to choose the baby's name and it was overwhelmingly voted that if it was a girl it would be called Toyah and if it was a boy it would be called Marilyn. The State sponsored christening was organized by the Pope's agent Deutschmark McCormack, who arranged font water by Perrier, nappies by Lacoste and the Archbishop of Canterbury's robes by Gucci. The religious ceremony was followed by the McCormack-Pope John-Bob Hope-Queen Elizabeth II World Invitation Open Golf Tennis Championship in the grounds of Buckingham Palace, or Nissan House as it was now called. In the sudden-death play-off, the baby's grandfather and his Uncle Andrew were the winners, following the sudden deaths of Roddy Lewellyn, Nigel Dempster and the entire staff of William Hickey.

CHAPTER 37

THE FUTURE.

The Masterplan was working well in the eighties. With Big Mother watching, with five hundred businesses great and small going bankrupt each week, with a jolly good row going on the Common Market, whose other members were all too common for Big Mother's liking, with four million out of work, with the unions demoralized and Britain's providential good luck in finally not managing to win a single Oscar in 1984 and, even more fortuitously, failing also to win the Eurovision Song Contest, the process of hoodwinking the world into believing that we were no longer Top Nation was now complete.

Britain knew better.

TEST PAPER IV

1) 'The De Lorean Car is not to be sniffed at.' Explain.

    (*Use the real thing.*)

2) Who said 'It's quicker by Tube':
    a) The Head of London Transport?
    b) The brewer of Foster's Lager?
    c) The mother of Louise Brown?

    (*Be fertile.*)

3) How shall history remember Britt Ekland, as:
    i) A minor film actress?
    ii) The wife of Rod Stewart?
    iii) The Youth Opportunities Programme?

4) Who fought over the cod pieces? Was it:
    a) Captain Kirk on the Danish trawler *Staadrek*?
    b) Customers at Bejam's summer sale?
    c) Balletomanes at an auction of Rudolf Nureyev's special effects?

    (*Be deceiving.*)

5) Cliff Richard was said to be 'seriously considering marriage'. How does this statement compare with the following: 'Pope John is seriously considering divorce.'

(*Be fanciful.*)

6) Was a Tebbit:
   i) A Lord of the Rings?
   ii) An outmoded form of bicycle?
   iii) A semi-house-trained polecat?

7) Arthur Scargill, the miners' leader, called a number of famous miners' rallies. Were these held at:
   a) Durham?
   b) Nottingham?
   c) Nuremberg?

(*Be militant.*)

8) Prince William, the son of the Prince and Princess of Wales, is descended from an ancient British King. Was he:
   i) Egbert?
   ii) Bacon and Eggbert?
   iii) Sausauge Chips and Egbert?

(*Be greasy.*)

9) Mrs Thatcher was said to be keen on preserving the House of Lords. Which method did she prefer:
   a) Constitutional reform?
   b) Formaldehyde?
   c) Embalming?

10) In the fifties, Senator McCarthy thought it 'Better dead than Red'. In the eighties, who said 'Better Red than Dead':
   i) The Greenham Common Women?
   ii) Liverpool Labour Group?
   iii) Precedent Raygun's hairdresser?

   (Don't dye in the attempt.)

11) In the eighties, what would you give the man who had everything:
   a) A platinum American Express Card?
   b) A personal communications satellite?
   c) Penicillin?

12) President Mitterand said of Mrs Thatcher: 'She must be the first woman in history to withdraw.' Explain.

13) How many people were involved in the film of the Dallas herpes disaster, 'The Texas Cold Sore Massacre'?

   (No artificial AIDS may be used.)

14) The Review of the Fleet was relocated in the eighties. Was it held at:
   i) The Thames Barrage?
   ii) The Solent?
   iii) The Serpentine?

15) Was the Sporting Person of the Decade:
   a) Torvill or Dean?

141

b) Zola Budd?
c) Joan Collins?

> (*Keep it up for as long as you can.*)

16) Which was the most popular diet book of the decade:
   i) The Noël Coward 'I have a Talent to A-Muesli' book?
   ii) The Scargill Diet?
   iii) The Beverly Sills Diet for Opera Singers Whose Great Fat Hands Are Frozen?

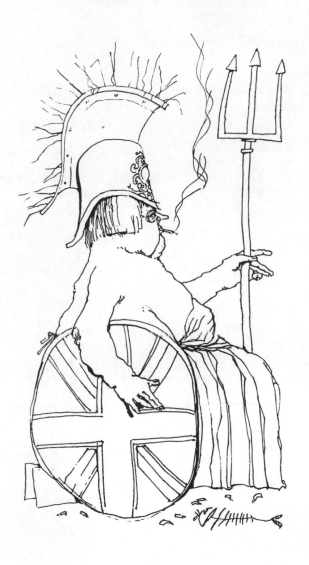